MUTT
DOG!

For all scruffy Mutts.

S.M.K.

Other books by
STEPHEN MICHAEL KING:

WORDS AND PICTURES:

The Man Who Loved Boxes
Patricia
Henry and Amy
Emily Loves to Bounce
Milli, Jack and the Dancing Cat

PICTURES:

Beetle Soup
The Little Blue Parcel
Amelia Ellicott's Garden
Pocket Dogs
Where Does Thursday Go?
Piglet and Mama

Scholastic Press
345 Pacific Highway
Lindfield NSW 2070
An imprint of Scholastic Australia Pty Limited (ABN 11 000 614 577)
PO Box 579
Gosford NSW 2250
www.scholastic.com.au

Part of the Scholastic Group
Sydney ● Auckland ● New York ● Toronto ● London ● Mexico City
● New Delhi ● Hong Kong ● Buenos Aires ● Puerto Rico

0-439-79216-9
This edition first printing, Sept. 2005
Text and illustrations copyright © Stephen Michael King, 2004.

Typeset in Mothergoose.

Printed by Tien Wah Press, Singapore

10 9 8 7 6 5 4 3 2 1   4 5 6 7 8 / 0

Thanks to Trish, Tanith, Luka, Muttley Christmas, Milli, Peppermint, Coco, Margaret Connolly, Margrete Lamond and my sister Mel.

MUTT

WORDS AND PICTURES Stephen Michael King

DOG!

In the city lived a dog . . .

who belonged to no-one.

He had to be brave,

and fast,

and smart . . .

just to survive.

He ate whatever he could find.

And looked for a new place to sleep . . .

every night.

One evening he found a halfway house.

Inside there were people

who were cold

and tired . . .

like him.

There wasn't enough room . . .
or even enough food for a dog.

A lady who worked there
tried to put him outside

but the scruffy dog
wiggled free . . .

and hid in a corner.

What am I going
to do with you?

She gave him a biscuit . . .

and made him a bed.

The next morning,
he was on his way . . .

This is no place
for a stray dog.

I wish you
could stay.

The sky was black and his stomach felt empty.

He looked for breakfast,

and a new place to sleep.

'Wait! Scruffy dog!'
called a voice.

Would you like
to come home
with me?

It was the lady from
the halfway house.

They left the city, and the air filled with new smells.

His new family gave him the first bath he'd ever had.

They brushed out
his matted knots,

gave him food from
a big tin can . . .

and something
delicious to chew.

Everyone thought up all sorts of names —

Bear,

Winston,

Tyrone,

Radiator,

Piccasso,

Fly,

Sigmund,

Heathcliff,

Errol,

Splot

Dingo,

Dustin,

Affro,

Dredd!

But most of the time everyone called him . . .

Mutt Dog!

Who's a
lucky little
Mutt Dog?

Mutt Dog
is brave,

and fast,

and smart.

He's gentle and loyal,

and each night when he goes to sleep . . .

. . . he knows where he belongs.